BARNEY THE PIRATE

Boisterous Books

FOR MICHAEL

First Published 2014
by *Boisterous Books Ltd*
in an edition of 200,
of which this is number 71

British Library Cataloguing
in Publication Data.
A catalogue record for this book
is available from the British Library.

ISBN 978-0-9930936-0-9

Text copyright © Jess Webb
Illustrations © Tony Kerins
Designed by Mark Foster

Printed by Henry Ling Limited

www.**boisterousbooks**.com

Barney the Pirate

by Jess Webb and Tony Kerins

BARNEY WAS A BEAUTIFUL BABY – quite bald.
His parents, Black-haired Jake, the pirate, and his
mother Aggie, the piratess, loved him to bits.

They gave him the best of everything and he
flourished on their ship *The Horrible Halibut*.
As soon as he had teeth, he enjoyed
chewing on rubbery rings of squid.
And he loved fish fingers.

HIS HAIR started to grow and
by the time he was celebrating
his first birthday, he had a fine
head of black, curly hair,
just like his father.

THERE WAS NEVER ANY DOUBT that he would follow in his father's footsteps and become a pirate-first-class. He passed all the necessary exams and always came top of the class. So, by the time he was 21, he was ready to accompany his father on boarding raids at sea.

HE LOVED BEING A JOLLY PIRATE and when Jake and Aggie retired to their houseboat, The Dunpillaging, Barney became captain of the The Horrible Halibut. He and his crew were the most feared on the high seas.

BUT HE WAS VERY DISMAYED to discover, one Tuesday afternoon, that he had a bald spot at the back of his head.

THE YEARS PASSED but a big shadow hung over Barney,
spoiling his otherwise happy life; he could no longer
ignore the fact that he was now completely bald,
and although he had a long, black, curly beard
and a very hairy chest he could not
find a single hair on his head.

He tried all the hair restorers that he knew of: Mermaid's Mousse, Turtle's Tonic and Seaweed Shampoo – but to no avail – nothing worked. He had given up all hope of restoring his head to even a few black hairs and was sitting on the deck of *The Horrible Halibut* one sunny afternoon – I think it was a Friday – when something happened to change his life!

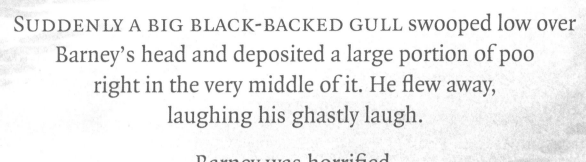

SUDDENLY A BIG BLACK-BACKED GULL swooped low over Barney's head and deposited a large portion of poo right in the very middle of it. He flew away, laughing his ghastly laugh.

Barney was horrified.

'I know this is supposed to be lucky, but I don't need it – it's the last straw.'

BARNEY WAS TOO FED UP to wash himself that night – he just couldn't be bothered. But in the morning he got up, full of resolution. He would wear a wig!

However, whilst in the shower and singing *'What shall we do with the drunken sailor'* at the top of his voice, something amazing happened. He was paying particular attention to the spot on his head where the gull had left the poo when he felt a little prickling sensation. Barney couldn't believe it. What could it be?

Maybe you've guessed. It was new hair! Day after day the few little prickles turned into proper black, curly hair – just like Barney used to have.

NOW, ALTHOUGH BARNEY WAS VERY HAPPY with his new head of hair, he soon realised that he must take steps to ensure that it didn't start falling out again. So he decided he would try and make a hair restorer using the very material that had restored his own hair – seagull poo!

He asked all his mates to collect what they could from the rocks and cliffs around. He paid them well and, although they thought he was bonkers, they soon brought him several barrels of the stuff. It was very smelly.

'OK,' said Barney, 'it is rather pongy. What can I do to make it smell good?'

HE STUDIED all his books about flowers and their fragrances and after a few experiments settled on a small blue flower which grew in abundance on a nearby hill; I can't tell you the name because it has to be a secret.

BARNEY TOOK ADVICE from an eccentric (ask someone what that means) old friend of his father who had a laboratory, and made up a mixture of poo and blue flowers (the name must remain secret).

He tried a small sample on his own head. He was delighted to find his hair growing even stronger and more beautiful than ever. 'Eureka!' he shouted. 'This could make me a fortune.'

What should he call it? Have you got any ideas? So he ran a little competition in the local paper and came up with the name *Mariner's Miracle Mixture*.

Of course it had to be bottled in some way and when he looked through the many jars and bottles he had collected over the years he found one shaped like a barrel – just the job!

So Barney forgot about being a pirate and became a businessman selling his hair restorer to the big shops and hairdressers over all the West Country. He even took on a couple of salesmen to meet the demand.

THINGS WERE GOING VERY WELL for Barney's business.
There was no shortage of poo and blue flowers (I still can't
tell you the name). He made lots of money but there was
no *special someone* in his life to spend it on!

HE WAS HAVING SUNDAY LUNCH with his parents one day – he still liked fish fingers but now had them with a delicious oyster sauce. When he looked at his mum and dad, still in love after many years, he realised that he must make an effort to find that *special someone* with whom he could spend the rest of his life – and his fortune!

BUT HOW COULD HE FIND HER? What about a dating agency?

A bit risky, perhaps. Or should he put an *ad* in the dating column in the local paper?

Then he decided to keep things simple and wrote a card to put in one of the local shops.

With no more ado he hastened to the newsagent on the corner and asked the nice lady to put his card in the window for a couple of weeks, which she did with a smile. He picked up his copy of *Fishing News*, paid the nice lady and left the shop, humming a sea shanty as he went.

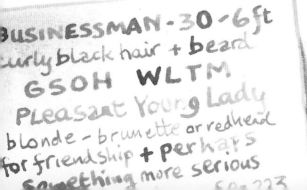

BUSINESSMAN · 30 · 6ft
curly black hair + beard
GSOH   WLTM.
Pleasant Young Lady
blonde – brunette or redhead
for friendship + perhaps
something more serious

BARNEY WAITED BY THE PHONE for several days but the longed-for call did not come. Then one Thursday the telephone rang.

A young lady, 23, introduced herself as Belinda and told Barney that when she went into the newsagent to pick up her copy of 50 *Ways with Fish*, she stopped to look at the cards in the window. The nice lady was just taking them out because the two weeks were up. But being a nice lady and a bit of a match-maker she showed Belinda Barney's card. Belinda made a note of the phone number and had now plucked up courage to ring. She had a lovely mellifluous voice (ask someone!) and she and Barney immediately felt comfortable with each other. Not wishing to delay the meeting they arranged to see each other at *The Old Lobster Pot* the very next day.

So at three o'clock on Friday, Barney was waiting at a table for two where he could see everyone who came in.

JUST AS THE CLOCK STRUCK THREE, the door opened, a shaft of golden light streamed in and there was this lovely young lady! She smiled at Barney (her smile was like sun shining through the clouds on an April day). Then she came to meet him. Barney was dumb-struck. As he stood to greet her, he could hear an angel choir singing 'Alleluia'.

When he finally found his voice, they sat down to tea and scones and talked for ages. In fact they had to leave at six o'clock because *The Old Lobster Pot* was closing.

WELL, THERE'S NO DOUBT that it was
LOVE AT FIRST SIGHT –
they had each found their soul-mate.
There's not much more to tell.
No point in a long engagement
because they were both quite sure
that marriage was their goal.
Where to have the ceremony?
On the beach, perhaps?
No – the tide might come in
at the wrong moment.

SO THEY WENT TO SEE THE VICAR at the lovely little chapel on the cliffs and he agreed to marry them at two o'clock on St Valentine's Day. It fell on a Saturday that year. It was a beautiful day – sunny but not too hot and Belinda looked gorgeous in her silk dress decorated with real pearls. Her bouquet was a mass of those blue flowers; the name of them is still a secret, I'm afraid.

AS THEY LEAVE THE CHURCH, spare a thought for the mummy black-backed gull sitting on her three eggs on the nest perched precariously on a narrow ledge high up on the cliff.

Of course, they lived happily ever after!

The End

Oh, I nearly forgot to tell you.
On Christmas Day, Santa had another chimney
to add to his list. Baby Benjy had arrived
on Christmas Eve.
He was a beautiful baby boy – quite bald.